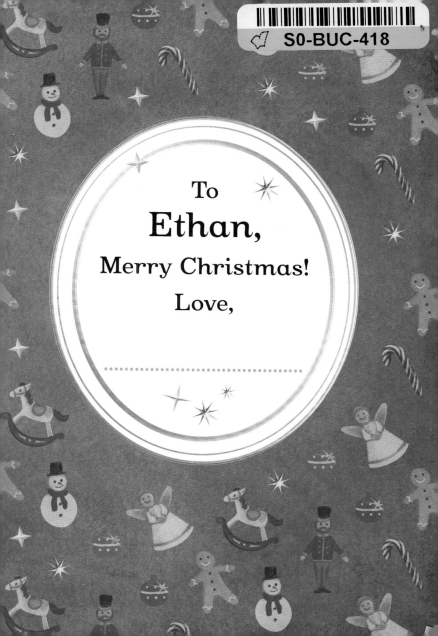

To
Ethan,
Merry Christmas!
Love,

....

'Twas the night before Christmas,
when all through the house,
Not a creature was stirring,
not even a mouse;
Ethan's stocking was hung
by the chimney with care,
In hope that St. Nicholas
soon would be there.

Ethan was nestled all snug in his bed,
While visions of candy canes danced in his head.
And Mom in her kerchief, and Dad in his cap,
Had just settled down for a long winter's nap.

When out on the street
there arose such a clatter,
Ethan sprang from his bed
to see what was the matter.
Away to the window
Ethan flew like a flash,
Tore open the curtains,
threw open the latch.

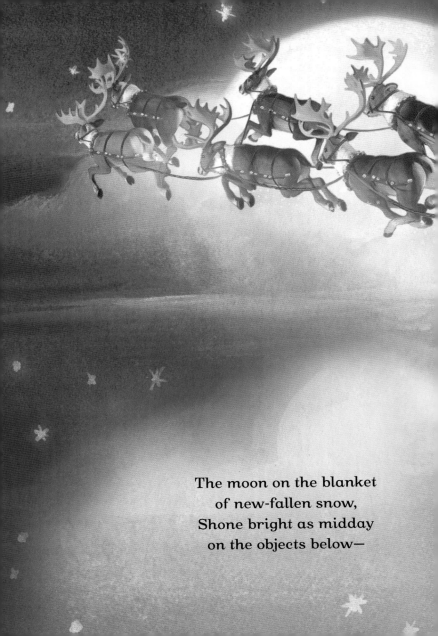

The moon on the blanket
of new-fallen snow,
Shone bright as midday
on the objects below—

To
Ethan

When, what to Ethan's
wondering eyes should appear,
But a miniature sleigh
and eight tiny reindeer.

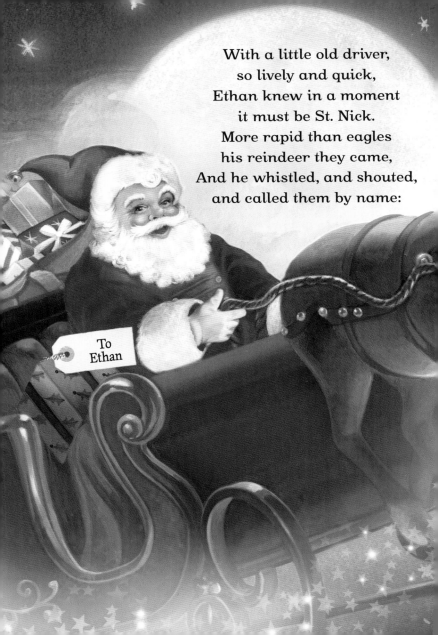

With a little old driver,
so lively and quick,
Ethan knew in a moment
it must be St. Nick.
More rapid than eagles
his reindeer they came,
And he whistled, and shouted,
and called them by name:

To
Ethan

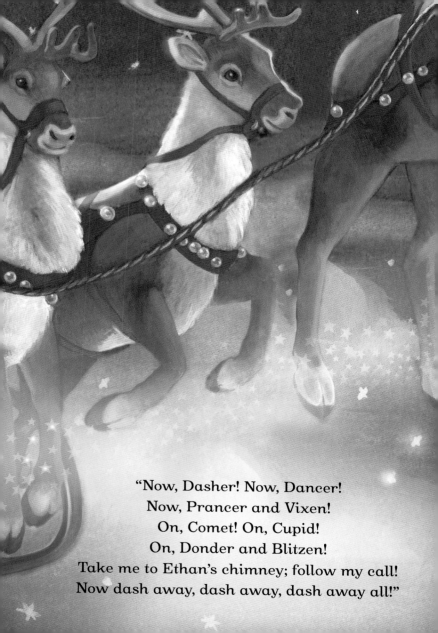

"Now, Dasher! Now, Dancer!
Now, Prancer and Vixen!
On, Comet! On, Cupid!
On, Donder and Blitzen!
Take me to Ethan's chimney; follow my call!
Now dash away, dash away, dash away all!"

And then, in a twinkling,
Ethan heard on the roof
The prancing and pawing
of each little hoof.

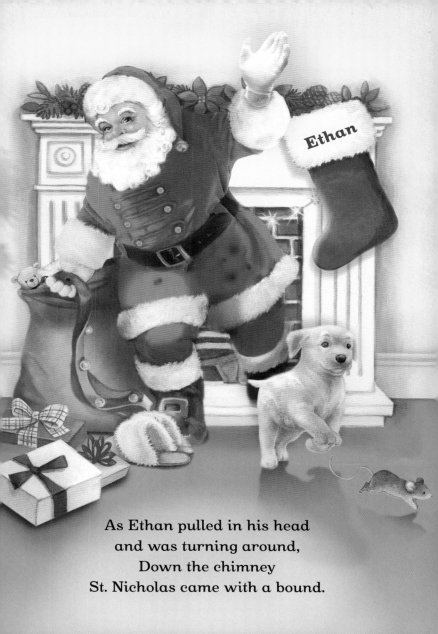

As Ethan pulled in his head
and was turning around,
Down the chimney
St. Nicholas came with a bound.

He was dressed all in fur,
from his head to his foot,
And his clothes were all tarnished
with ashes and soot.
A bundle of toys he had
flung on his back,
And he looked like a peddler
holding his pack.

To
Ethan

His eyes—how they twinkled!
His dimples—how merry!
His cheeks were like roses,
his nose like a cherry.
His droll little mouth
was drawn up like a bow,
And the beard on his chin was
as white as the snow.

Dear Santa,
I hope you enjoy
the sweet treats.
Love,
Ethan
P.S. The carrots
are for your
furry friends.

A big sack of toys
he held tight in his fist,
And he glanced to see Ethan
on top of his list.
He had a broad face
and a little round belly
That shook when he laughed,
like a bowl full of jelly.

Ethan

NICE LIST
Ethan
Steven
Glenn
Marcus
Lorenzo

He was chubby and plump,
a right jolly old elf,
And Ethan laughed when he saw him,
in spite of himself.

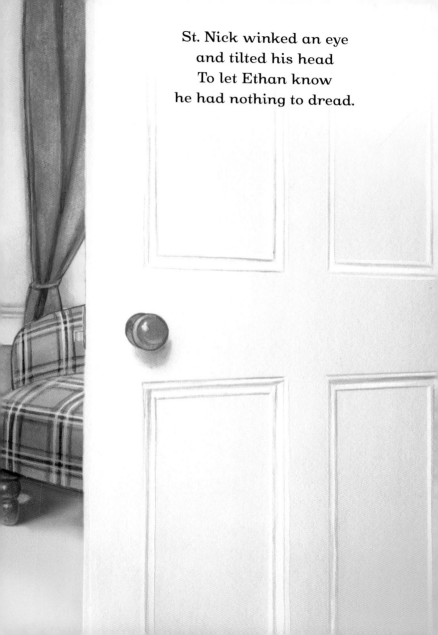

St. Nick winked an eye
and tilted his head
To let Ethan know
he had nothing to dread.

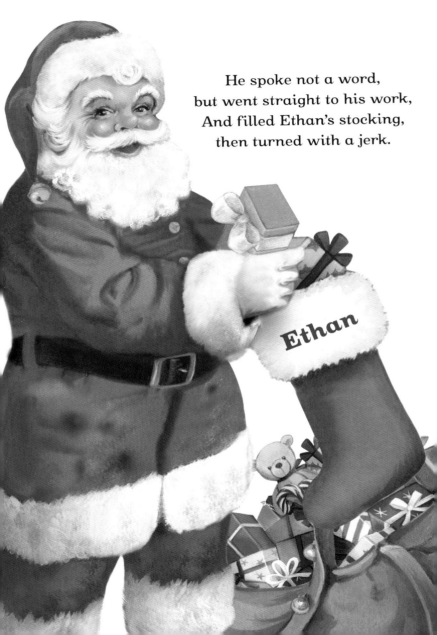

He spoke not a word,
but went straight to his work,
And filled Ethan's stocking,
then turned with a jerk.

And tapping his finger at the side of his nose,
And giving a nod, up the chimney he rose.

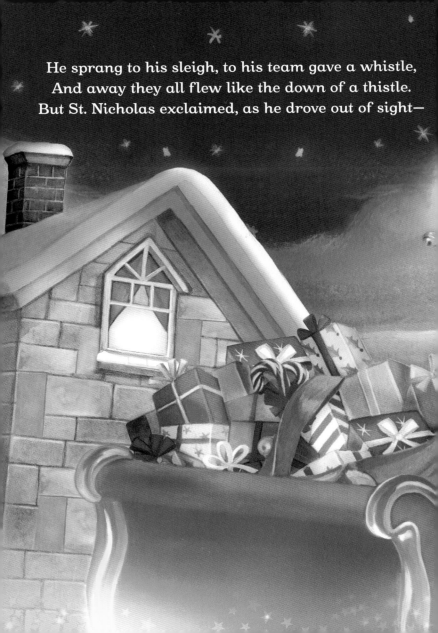

He sprang to his sleigh, to his team gave a whistle,
And away they all flew like the down of a thistle.
But St. Nicholas exclaimed, as he drove out of sight—

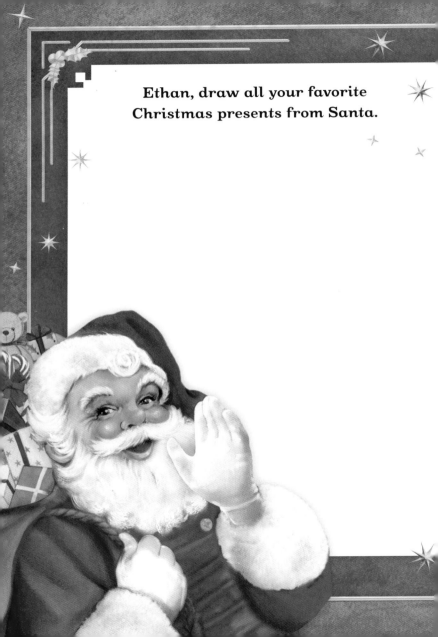

**Ethan, draw all your favorite
Christmas presents from Santa.**

Adapted from the poem by Clement C. Moore
Illustrated by Lisa Alderson
Designed by Jane Gollner

Published by Put Me In The Story,
a publication of Sourcebooks, Inc.
P.O. Box 4410, Naperville, Illinois 60567-4410
(630) 536-1104
www.putmeinthestory.com

Date of Production: July 2019
Run Number: 5015191
Printed and bound in Italy (LG)
10 9 8 7 6 5 4 3 2 1

FSC
www.fsc.org

MIX
Paper from
responsible sources
FSC® C023419

put me
in the story®
Bestselling books starring your child!
www.putmeinthestory.com